To my dad and grandpa.
— Ellen DeLange

To my family, who support me in all possible ways.
— Zafouko Yamamoto

Originally published as *Wie kwettert mij wakker?* in Belgium and the Netherlands by Clavis Uitgeverij, 2020
English translation from the Dutch by Clavis Publishing Inc., New York

Visit us on the Web at www.clavis-publishing.com.

Who Is Shrieking So Early? written by Ellen DeLange and illustrated by Zafouko Yamamoto

ISBN 978-1-60537-591-5

This book was printed in December 2020 at Nikara, M. R. Štefánika 858/25, 963 01 Krupina, Slovakia.

First Edition
10 9 8 7 6 5 4 3 2 1

Who Is SHRIEKING So Early?

Written by **Ellen DeLange**
Illustrated by **Zafouko Yamamoto**

Clavis

NEW YORK

Early one morning, just before the alarm clock is
about to go off, a strange sound enters the bedroom . . .

SHRIEK
SHRIEK

Startled, Sam sits straight up in his bed.
What's happening? What's that noise?

Sam slips out of bed and quickly climbs on a chair to look outside. He notices a bird in the tree next to his bedroom window.

Sam opens the window and calls out: "Go away, I want to **wake up** quietly! This isn't a good way to start my day!" Sam's dog has jumped off the bed as well, barking loudly.

The bird doesn't listen to Sam, or his dog . . .
Whatever Sam tries, he can't escape the loud
shrieking sound of the bird.
"I hope it doesn't show up tomorrow morning,"
sighs Sam, deeply hidden under his blanket.

The noise is even louder the next morning.
"Oh no, not again! What else can I do to stop it?
I've already tried so many different things."

He opens the window and yells: "Go away!
Don't **wake** me **up** with your awful noise!"

SHRIEK
SHRIEK

The following morning it seems the bird
is gone. It's surprisingly quiet . . .
but it doesn't take long before
the noise starts again.

Sam runs outside,
wildly waving his arms.
"Stop it! Stop it!
Why don't you let me **wake
up** peacefully?" he shouts.

SHRIEK
SHRIEK

Sam has to come up with
a better plan.
What else can he possibly do
to scare the bird away?

Unfortunately, none of Sam's ideas are working.
He's close to losing his patience . . .

Sam walks into the backyard
to calm down. He needs some
quiet time to think about
what to do next.

"Annoying bird, why don't you let me
wake up quietly?" he says aloud.

"Have you tried to make friends with the bird?" says a voice on the other side of the hedge. "That might help," the voice continues. "Magpies can be very smart, you know."

Before Sam can respond, the man has already walked away.
Hey, he thinks, that might actually be a very good idea!
If we become friends, maybe the magpie will finally stop shrieking.

Sam runs back into the house, looking for food that he can feed to the magpie. All he can find are bread crumbs and dog kibbles. He takes a handful of both and runs back into the yard.

The magpie seems to like the food.
He even eats it from Sam's hand.

Unfortunately, feeding the bird
doesn't stop the shrieking.
Sam doesn't give up though.

"Please let me **wake up** quietly,"
he repeats every time he sees the bird.
"I know one day I'll find a way to stop
the shrieking," says Sam to his dog.

The dog has been patiently following
Sam around. He wags his tail
and carries his favorite toy. He tilts his
head as his big eyes plead with Sam.

"I can't play right now," says Sam,
"but you just gave me a great idea . . .
If I can teach you, maybe I can also
teach the bird . . ."

For days, Sam is busy training the magpie.
He teaches it to pick up garbage and even fetch a coin.

Sam is very happy with his new friend . . .
apart from the shrieking sound that wakes him up, of course.

Sam becomes more and more
attached to the bird. Every night
before going to bed, he opens
his bedroom window and says:
"Goodnight, bird! Can you please
let me **wake up** quietly tomorrow?"

Until one morning, as the sun rises, everything seems different;
more gentle and peaceful. There's no loud shrieking . . .
Instead Sam hears something totally different.

WAKE UP
WAKE UP

Can it be the magpie?

Sam runs outside as fast as he can.
"I knew you could do it!"
he says to his new friend.
"What a great way to start a new day!
Thank you, thank you!"

And what do you think the bird replied?

THANK YOU
THANK YOU